or outside, Percy loves spending time at his hut!

The hedgehog is sad –
his prickles will pop the balloons.

But wearing Percy's corks
.soon makes him happy again!

Percy's wheelbarrow
is **full** of tools...

But when it's empty,
there's time for a race!

Brrr! It's very cold
outside in the snow.

Luckily, the fox can wear Percy's **warm** clothes!

Oh no! Percy has lost
two buttons from his braces.

Can you see who has **found** them?

Oops! The owl has fallen
upside down
in her sleep!

That's better! Now she's the right way up.

Splash! Percy and his friends are **wet** after falling in the pond.

But everyone is soon **dry** again,
thanks to Percy's hairdryer!

The ducks climb
up the ladder...

and go down
the slide.
Whee!

A small acorn . . .

will grow into a
big oak tree!

The hedgehog is having
fun **on** the swing.

Uh oh! The rabbit has slipped **off** his swing. Watch out, everyone!

Percy is still **awake** when
a surprise visitor arrives.

Shh! Percy and the mole
are fast asleep.

Goodnight, everyone!

First published in paperback in the United Kingdom by HarperCollins *Children's Books* in 2022

1 3 5 7 9 10 8 6 4 2

ISBN: 978-0-00-853601-5

HarperCollins *Children's Books* is a division of HarperCollins*Publishers* Ltd
1 London Bridge Street, London SE1 9GF

www.harpercollins.co.uk

HarperCollins*Publishers*
1st Floor, Watermarque Building, Ringsend Road, Dublin 4, Ireland

Printed and bound in the UK